D1384729

A QUEEN IN JERUSALEM

KAR-BEN PUBLISHING, INC.
A division of Lerner Publishing Group, Inc.
241 First Avenue North
Minneapolis, MN 55401 USA
1-800-4-KARBEN
Website address: www.karben.com

Main body text set in Aptifer Slab LT Pro 15/20.
Typeface provided by Linotype AG.

Library of Congress Cataloging-in-Publication Data

The Cataloging-in-Publication Data for A Queen in Jerusalem is on file at the Library
of Congress.
ISBN 978-1-5124-4441-4 (lib. bdg.)
ISBN 978-1-5124-4442-1 (pbk.)
ISBN 978-1-5124-9845-5 (eb pdf)

Manufactured in the United States of America
1-42513-26190-5/18/2017

A QUEEN IN JERUSALEM

Tami Shem-Tov & Rachella Sandbank

Illustrated by **Avi Ofer**

Translated from the Hebrew by
Tirza Sandbank

KAR-BEN
PUBLISHING

TOMORROW IS PURIM AND MALKA DOESN'T HAVE A COSTUME.

"I hope it doesn't rain and get the laundry wet," says Malka's mother, hanging a shirt on the line.

But Malka hopes it will rain and get the laundry wet.

"You promised that this year you would make me a Queen Esther costume," says Malka angrily.

"I'm so sorry I didn't have time to make you a costume, Malka," says her mother wearily, "but you're a big girl now. You can make a costume yourself."

"But you promised me!" Malka is almost shouting. Her mother doesn't hear, because the baby has just woken up crying.

Malka runs out of the house,
banging the gate behind her.

In the streets of Jerusalem she can feel the holiday arriving. The air is filled with the scent of hamantaschen coming from the bakeries, and the streets are filled with excited children running around with groggers.

But Malka is sad. This Purim she will not have a beautiful crown, or a queen's scepter, or a robe woven with golden threads. She walks along quickly. It is cold and grey in the streets of Jerusalem and in Malka's heart.

Raindrops begin to fall.

Malka is deep in thought and doesn't pay attention to where she is going.

Suddenly she finds herself standing opposite a grey stone wall. She sees that the gate is open and just inside the gate sits a man, hammering on a stone and humming to himself as if the rain doesn't bother him.

He raises his eyes and looks at her.

"Hello," he says, "Can I help you? My name is Boris."

"I'm Malka," she replies.

"What a beautiful name!" says Boris.

Malka begins to cry.

"Don't you like your name?" asks Boris.
"Malka means 'queen,' a perfect name for Purim."

"That's just it," says Malka.

Malka sees Boris' kind eyes and tells him her story:
How her mother *promised* her that she would make
Malka a queen costume.
And how tomorrow is Purim and her mother was
too busy so Malka will not have a special Queen Esther
costume for the holiday.

"Well," smiles Boris, "you've come to the right place."

"What do you mean?" asks Malka in wonder, drying her tears.

"Follow me," he replies.

Boris opens a double door.

"These are our talented weavers," says Boris. Then he says to the weavers, "Quickly, everbody! We must create a robe for a queen!"

The smiling weavers crowd around Malka. They busily
measure, cut, sew and tie, and suddenly—magically—Malka is
wrapped in a long beautiful robe, woven with gold threads.

"Shall we continue?" smiles Boris offering her his arm.
They go on to the next hall; again full of people working.
"These are our talented goldsmiths," says Boris.
And to the goldsmiths he says, "We must create a regal scepter, and a crown inlaid with precious stones—and quickly please."

The goldsmiths huddle, consulting, taking bits of silver and tools from the drawers, and they get to work.

Malka watches as, before her eyes, a sheet of silver becomes
a crown and a royal scepter studded with precious stones.

Malka thinks she must be dreaming.

Boris places the crown on her head, and hands her the scepter.

"What is this place?" asks Malka.

"This is the Bezalel art school," explains Boris. "My students learn to draw, create sculptures, weave and do all sorts of crafts. Bezalel was the artist in the bible who helped design the Temple in Jerusalem two thousand years ago."

"And now, Malka, my queen, will you permit the Bezalel artists to paint pictures of you in your beautiful costume?" asks Boris. He leads a very excited Malka to yet another hall, and straight to a chair at the front of the room.

Malka sits in the chair, straight and queen-like, facing the art students. They look at her and paint. She has to keep still, and that is not easy, but a real queen knows how to behave.

When they are finished, Malka gets up to look at the paintings. She discovers that each artist has painted her slightly differently, and yet she can recognize herself in each of the paintings.

Boris walks Malka back to the gate.
"Before I came here to establish this art school," says
Boris, "I worked in the royal court of Bulgaria."

"Did you meet a real king and queen?" asks Malka excitedly.

"Oh yes," says Boris. "But now I have met a queen in Jerusalem as well," he adds, bowing to her.

"I hope that one day you will come back here as a student," says Boris.
Malka smiles and goes on her way, towards home.

It is cold, but nobody minds. Everyone stops to look at Malka.
There has never been a queen like this in the streets of Jerusalem.

Malka walks faster.

As she approaches her house, she starts running.

"Mommy," she cries, "look at me!"

AUTHOR'S NOTE

Malka, the heroine of this story, is the author's invention, but Boris Schatz was a real person—a sculptor and a painter, born in Russia in 1867. His dream was to open the first art school in Jerusalem; a place to study and create art, painting and sculpture, and other beautiful crafts like weaving and jewelry-making. Boris fulfilled his dream when, in 1906, he established Bezalel, an art school in Jerusalem which is still active today.

As a young man, Boris studied painting and sculpture in Russia and Paris. At first his work was unknown, but little by little he became known as an artist.

His sculpture of Judah Maccabee was exhibited at a big show in Paris. Important people from all over the world visited the exhibition, among them the king of Bulgaria who was so impressed by Boris' sculpture that he invited Boris to be the chief artist of the Bulgarian kingdom. Boris also founded a royal school of art in Bulgaria.

Boris then decided to establish an art school in Jerusalem. The Bezalel Academy of Arts and Design has existed in Jerusalem for more than a hundred years.